ZAZULEAC WORLD
Copyright
© Zazuleac World Inc.
All rights reserved

We hope you have a great experience with this book and we appreciate your support.

Connect With Us:

MISSING LETTERS

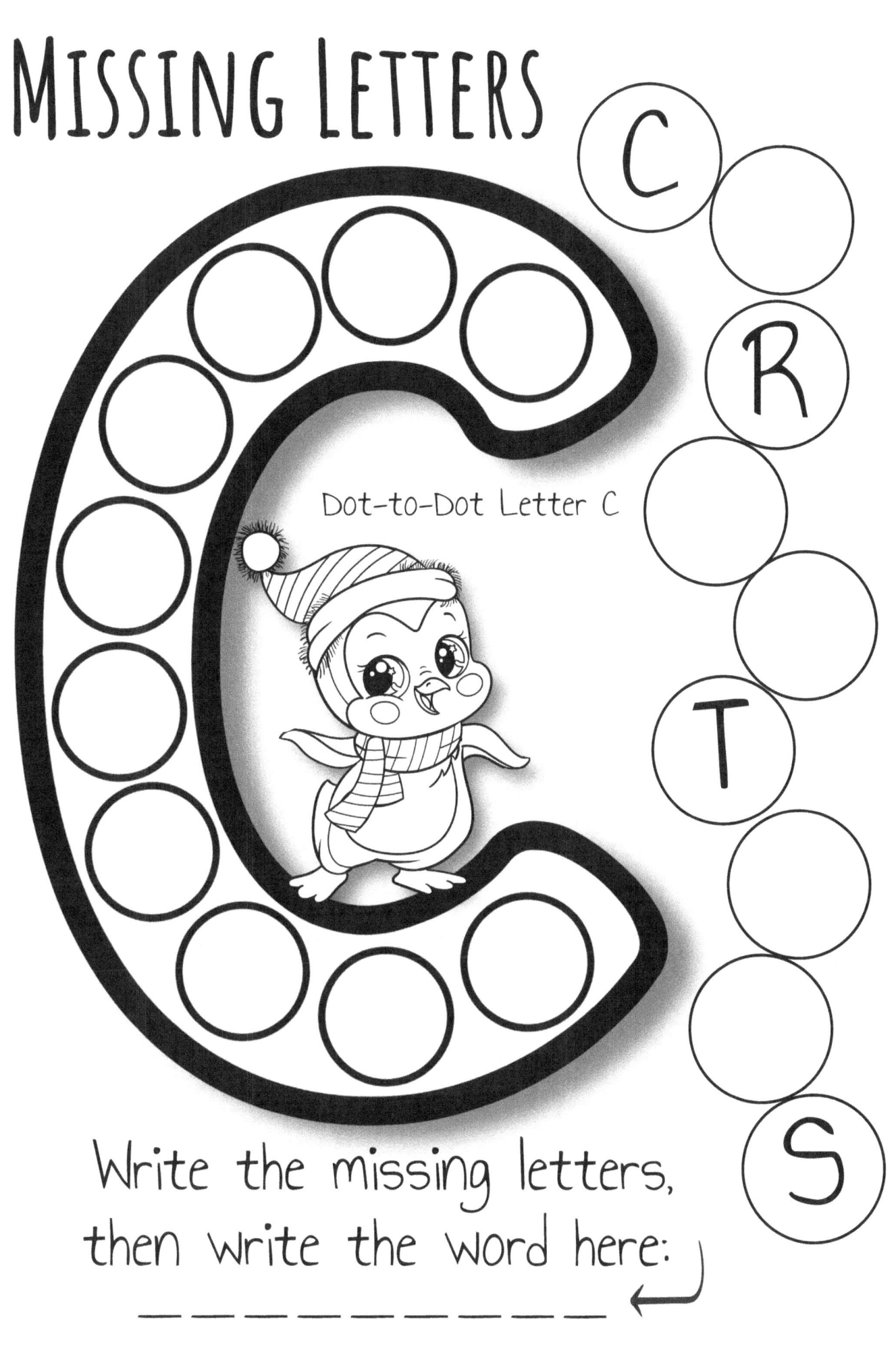

Dot-to-Dot Letter C

C

R

T

S

Write the missing letters, then write the word here:
_ _ _ _ _ _ _

CHRISTMAS ALPHABET

Write in the missing UPPERCASE letters

CHRISTMAS ALPHABET

Write in the missing lowercase letters

TRACING AND WRITING

Trace the following sentences and then
write it one more time on your own

Christmas time is fun

Holidays are here

December is my time

MISSING NUMBERS

Write in the square boxes the missing numbers

1		3		5	6			9	
				15					
									30
						37			
	42								
			54						
							68		
81									
				95					100

COUNTING BY 2'S

2   8   12

18

24

30

36

COUNTING BY 5'S

20

35

5

50

HOW MANY?
Count and circle the correct number

	① 1 ② 2 ③ 3		⑥ 6 ⑦ 7 ⑧ 8
	③ 3 ④ 4 ⑤ 5		⑦ 7 ⑧ 8 ⑨ 9
	④ 4 ⑤ 5 ⑥ 6		⑧ 8 ⑨ 9 ⑩ 10

PATTERNS

Cut and paste the correct picture to continue the pattern. Color the pictures

CONNECT THE DOTS

Color the pictures

ORNAMENT

Connect the number dots in order
Then, color the picture

SYMMETRY

Complete the other half of the picture
Color it

FIND THE DIFFERENCES

How many ?

A-Maze-ing Christmas

Help the bunny to find his friend

A-Maze-ing Friends

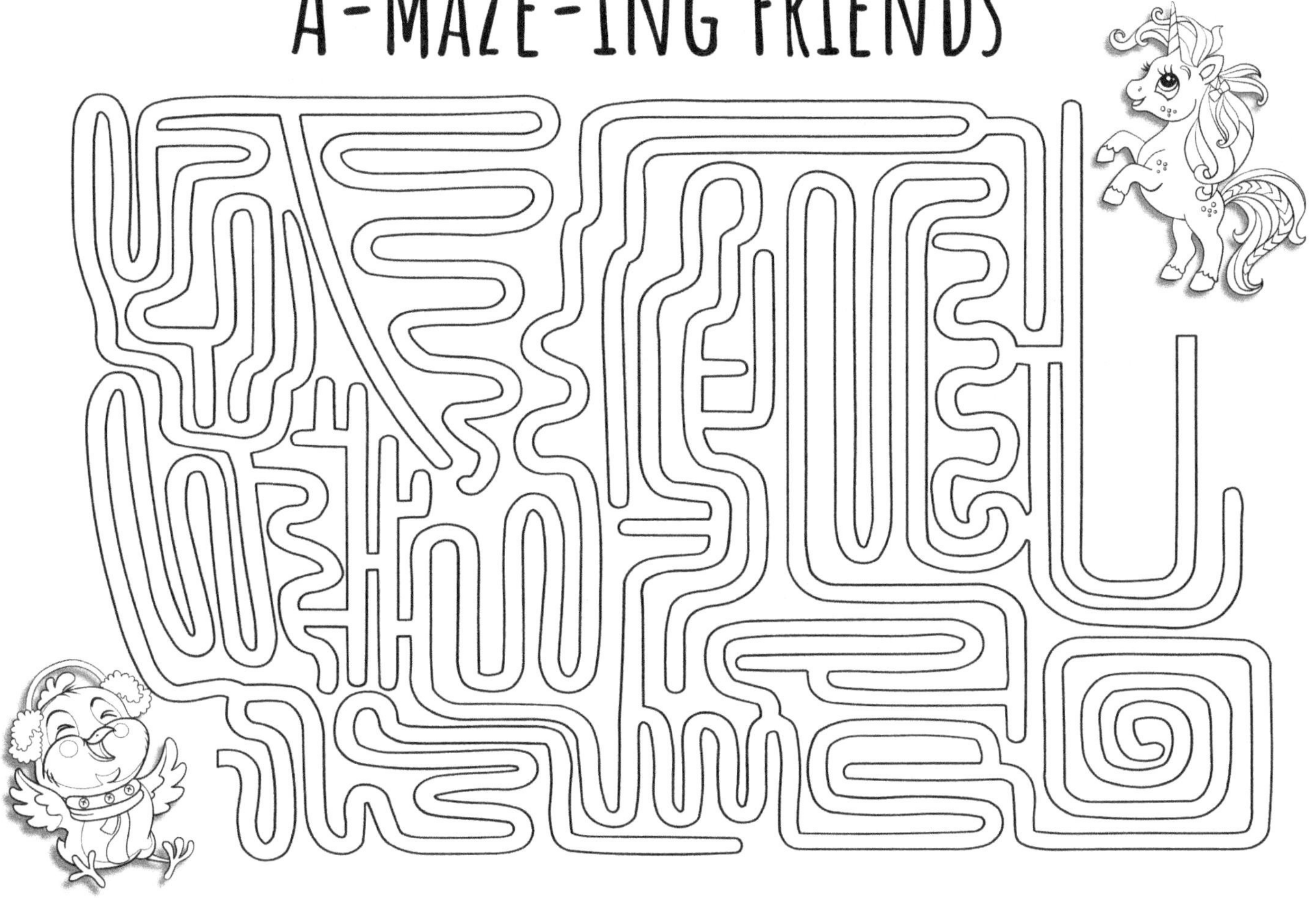

IGLOO LIFE

Which animals would most likely live in an igloo?
Circle them, then color them.

Gingerbread Man

The Gingerbread Man is a bit of a mess, can you help put him back together by cutting the pieces carefully?

PUZZLE GAME

Color the object inside the puzzle, then cut the puzzle and mix up the pieces. Make it up again and have fun

Ugly Sweater Design

Design and color a Christmas sweater

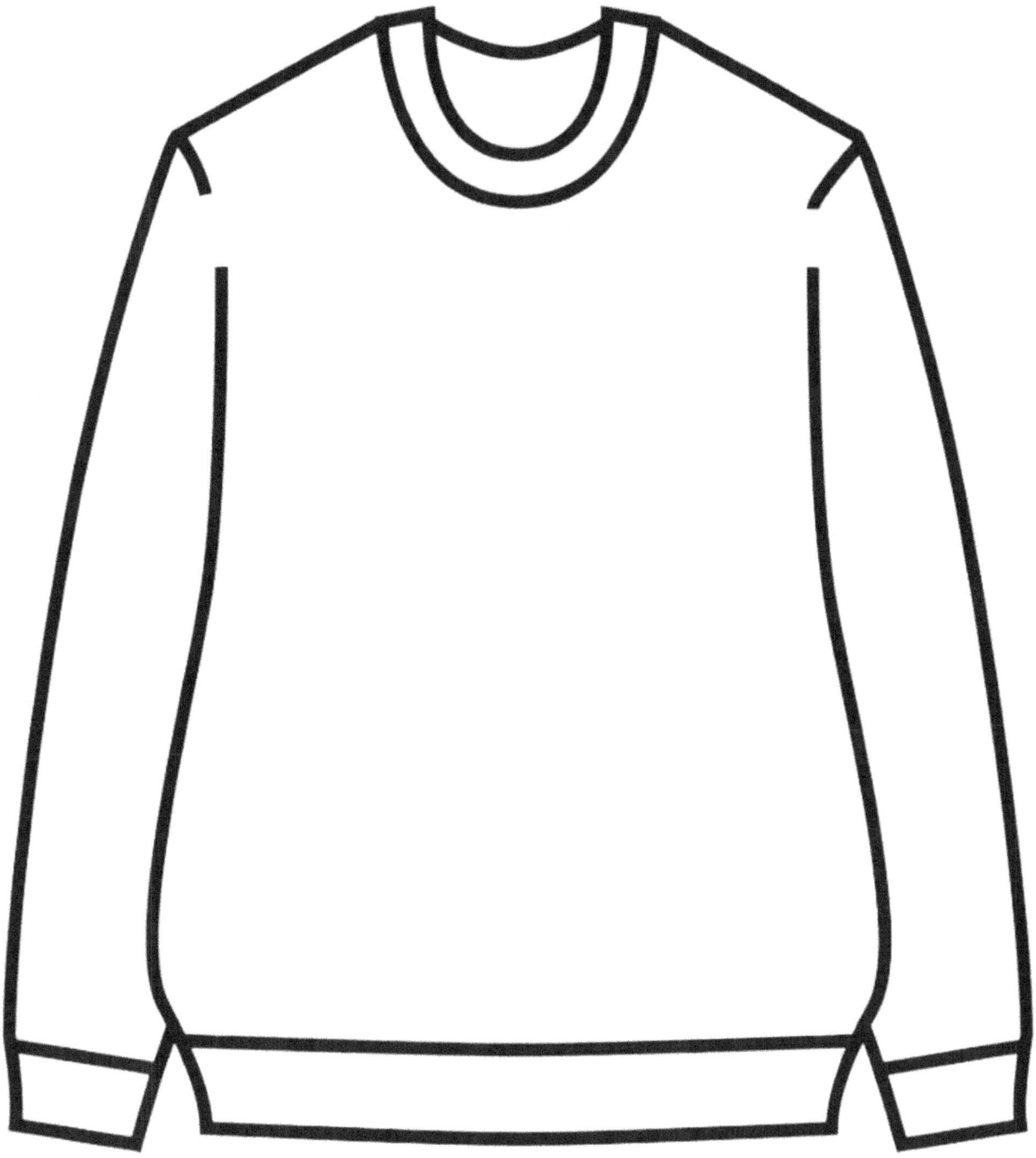

Build your Snowman

Color and complete the snowman pieces (see next page).
Add as many snowballs as the number of letters that make up your name
and write it on the snowman.

BUILD YOUR SNOWMAN
(part 2)

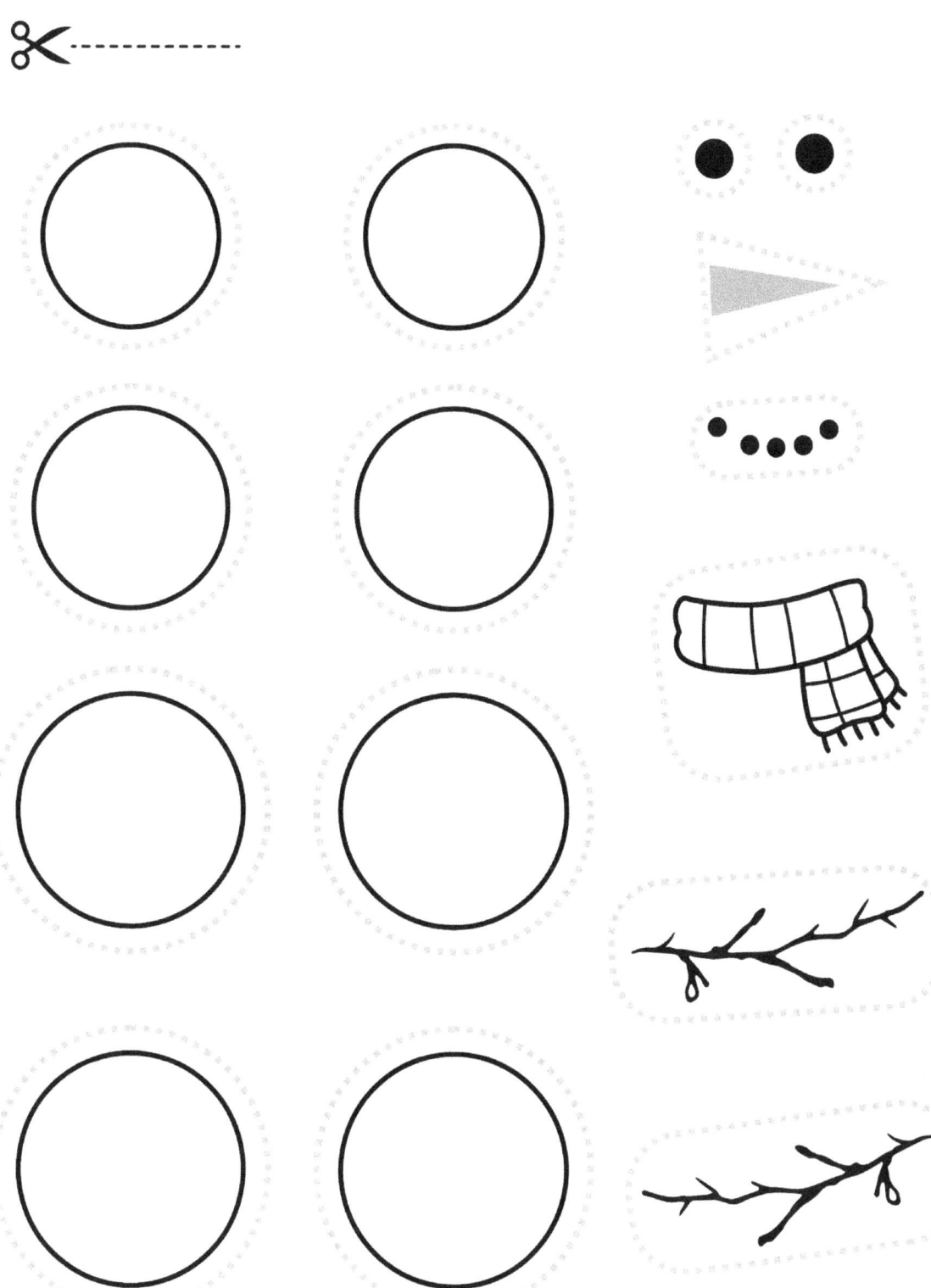

December Calendar

Build your calendar.

Write the dates and mark Christmas Day.

Monday	Tuesday	Wednesday	Thursday	Friday	Saturday	Sunday

DIPLODOCUS DECEMBER

To do list:

CHRISTMAS BOX

Color the box and the object inside of it. Then cut the box accordingly and get ready for presents.

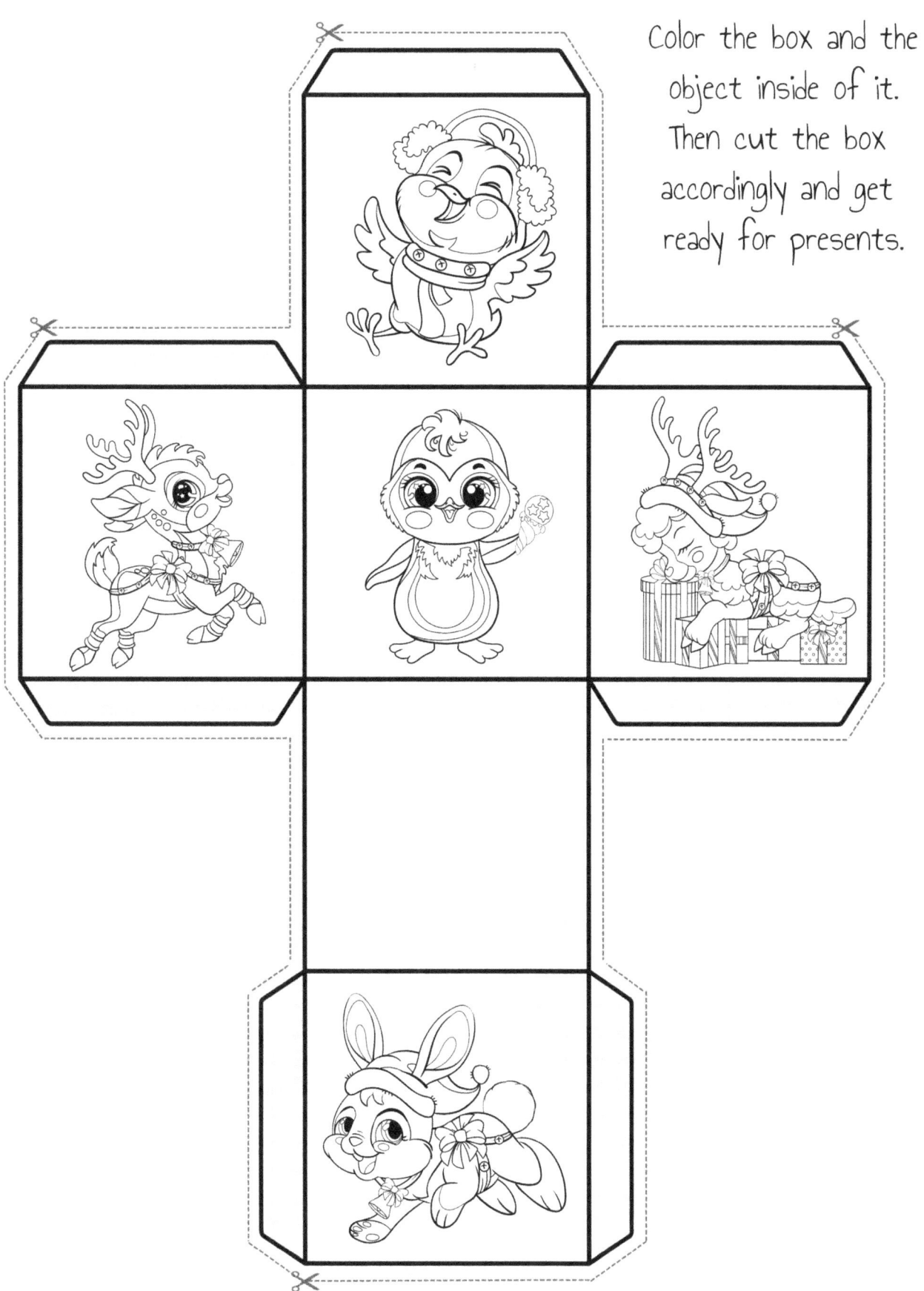

GRATEFUL

Inside each ornament write one thing you are grateful for this Christmas

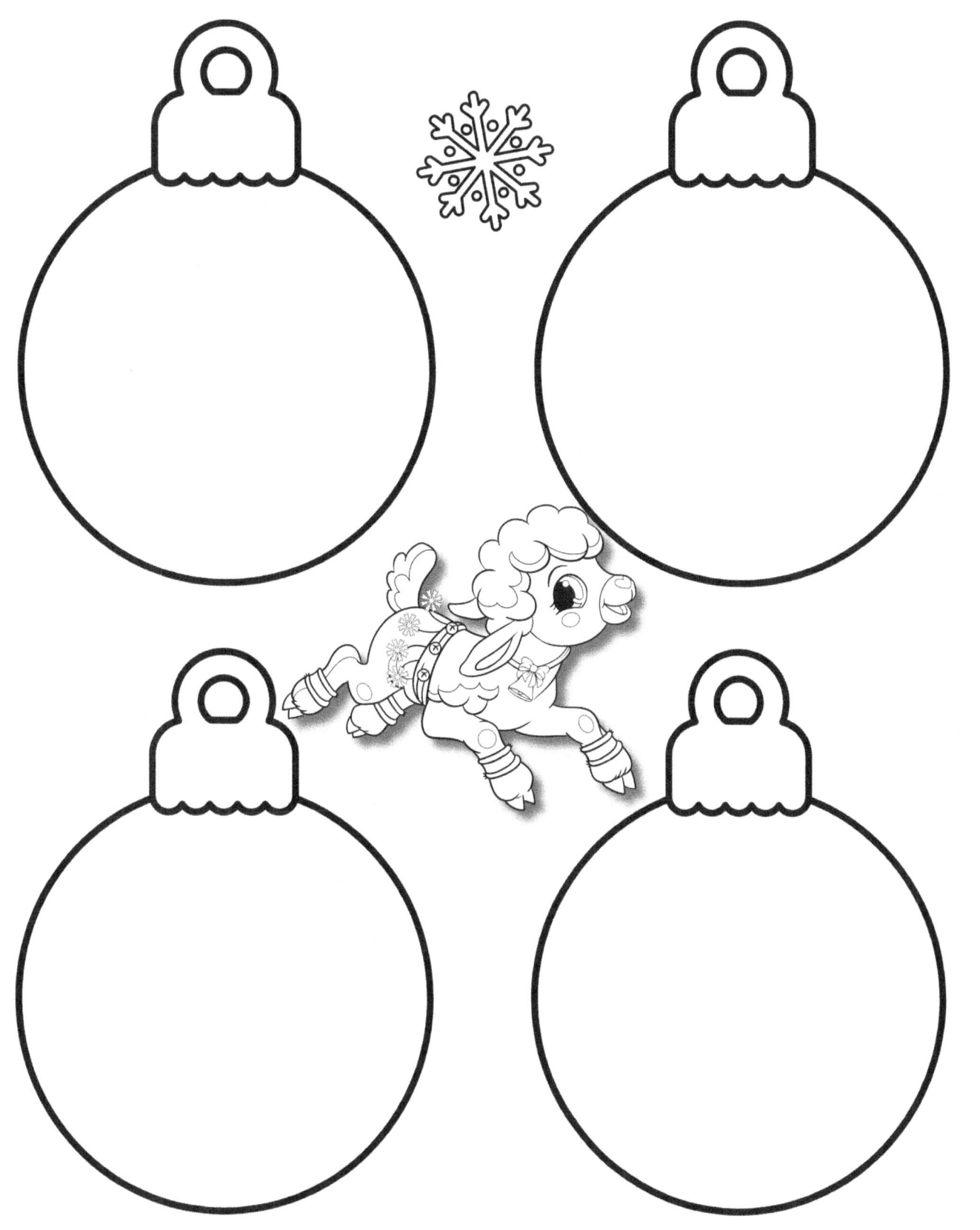

CHRISTMAS SNAPSHOTS

Draw or write your most memorable Christmas moments

Santa's Bag

Santa's bag with presents is here. Color the objects and write what presents would you love Santa to bring this Christmas?

Dear Santa

_____

_____

_____

_____

_____

_____

_____

_____

_____

CHRISTMAS BOOKMARKS